Library of Congress Cataloging-in-Publication Data
Carruth, George Albert.
The boy who loved birds / story by George Carruth; illustrations by Libby Carruth Krock.
p. cm.
Summary: A little boy dreams that he hatches form an egg with bird wings
and learns to fly. He eats, explore, meets a similar female bird and raises a bird family.
ISBN 0-9773167-0-X
[1.Birds--Fiction. 2.Nature--Fiction. 3.Imagination--Fiction.]
I. Krock, Libby Carruth, ill. II.Title.
PZ7.C19248 B6 2005
[E]--dc22   2005909666
Printed in China
First printing, April 2006
Reprinted, March 2007

The Boy Who Loved Birds

Revised Edition

story by George Carruth

illustrations by Libby Carruth Krock

Too Much Fun, LLC   Eastsound, WA

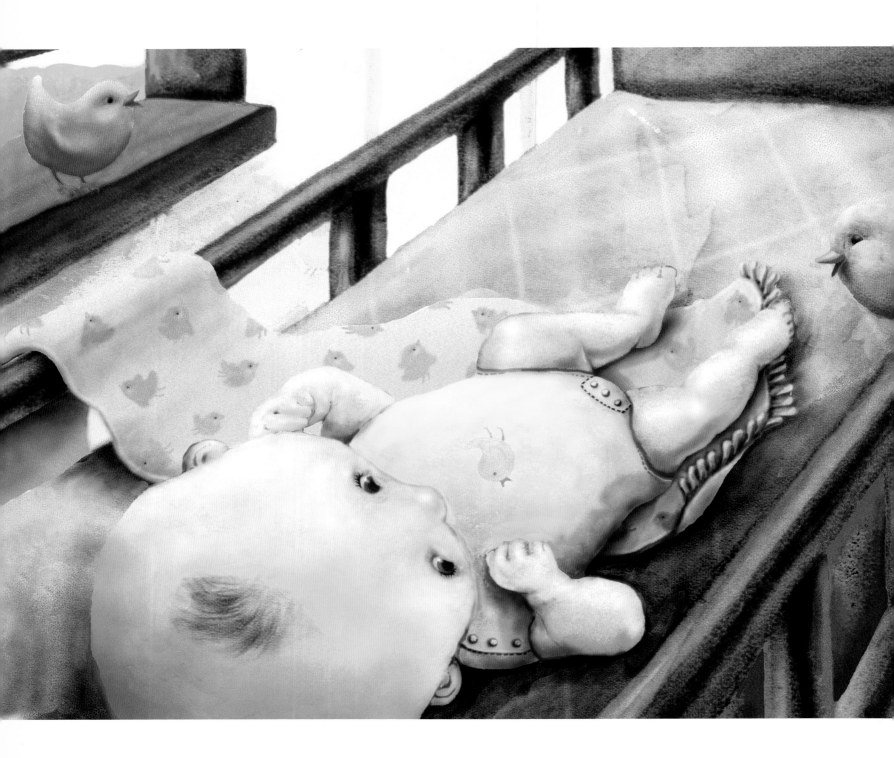

From the time
that he was just
a little baby,
this little boy
loved birds.

The boy loved birds
so much that he would
spend hours and hours
watching, listening to,
and even talking
with them.

His love for birds
was so strong that
almost every night
his dreams were filled
with colorful flying birds.

Blue birds, Red birds,
Yellow birds, Green birds,
Even Polkadot birds!

One night, something very strange and magical happened.

He dreamed that HE was a baby bird,
with his very own set of tiny colorful wings.
The only sound he could make
was a high-pitched "peep PEEP peep!"

But that was ok,
since baby birds
don't really need
other sounds.

Although he didn't
much care for the food
baby birds ate,

he continued to grow
bigger, stronger
and more colorful
every day.

Finally, the day came
when he was ready to
test his strong new wings.

Up and up
and higher and higher
he flew.

Follow the leader
became an everyday event.

Even when his friends
were tired of playing games,
he continued to fly throughout the night sky.

The air at nighttime was always so soft and cool,
and the town so very quiet and peaceful.

While soaring around
one beautiful warm
spring day,
something exciting
and unexpected happened!

There was a little girl!
And she had bright
colorful wings
just like his!

As time went by
they grew bigger and older.
Day after day was filled with
flying and talking
and laughing and flying!

Then one day,
guess what happened?

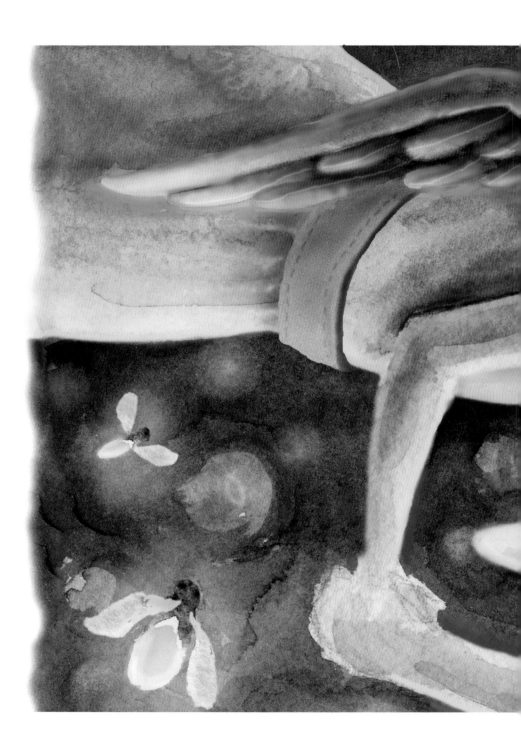

By the
following spring
something even more
wondrous and
exciting happened!

Mealtime was always an incredibly busy time for Mommy and Daddy birds.

Flying here and there, they collected juicy worms and crunchy grasshoppers for breakfast, juicy worms and crunchy grasshoppers for lunch, and juicy worms and crunchy grasshoppers for dinner!

Guess what they would eat for a bedtime snack?

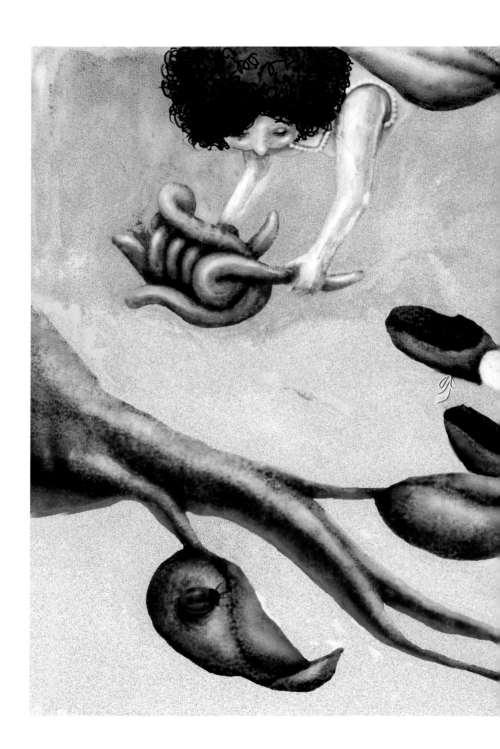

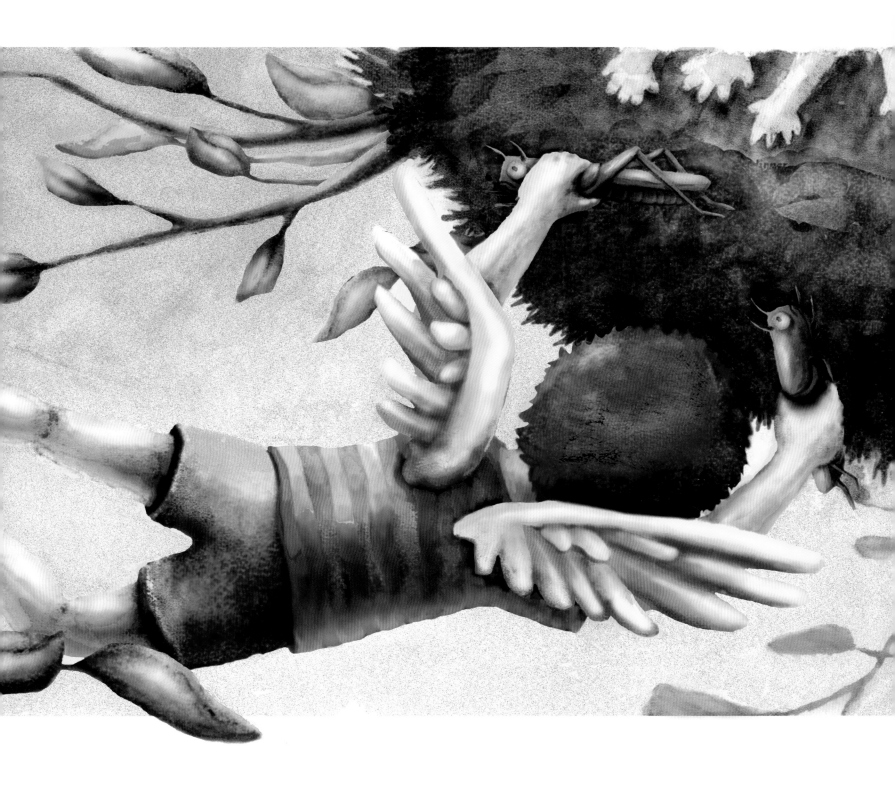

Juicy
worms
and
crunchy
grasshoppers!

The next morning
when the little boy awoke,
he remembered having
the most fabulous, fantastic
and amazing dream
of his life!

ring Ring

riNG

He dressed himself,
ate breakfast and ran outside
to tell his little neighbors
all about his
marvelous magical dream.

Chirping with delight,
they loved hearing every detail
of last night's
magical flying dream.
"Tell it again! Tell it again!"
they would chirp.

So over and over,
the little boy would
describe every detail as
his friends listened happily.

That evening as
he lay in bed,
the boy hoped his
dreams would be filled
with colorful birds
and girls with wings
and follow the leader
and juicy worms and
crunchy grasshoppers
and... ZZZZZZZ...

Z

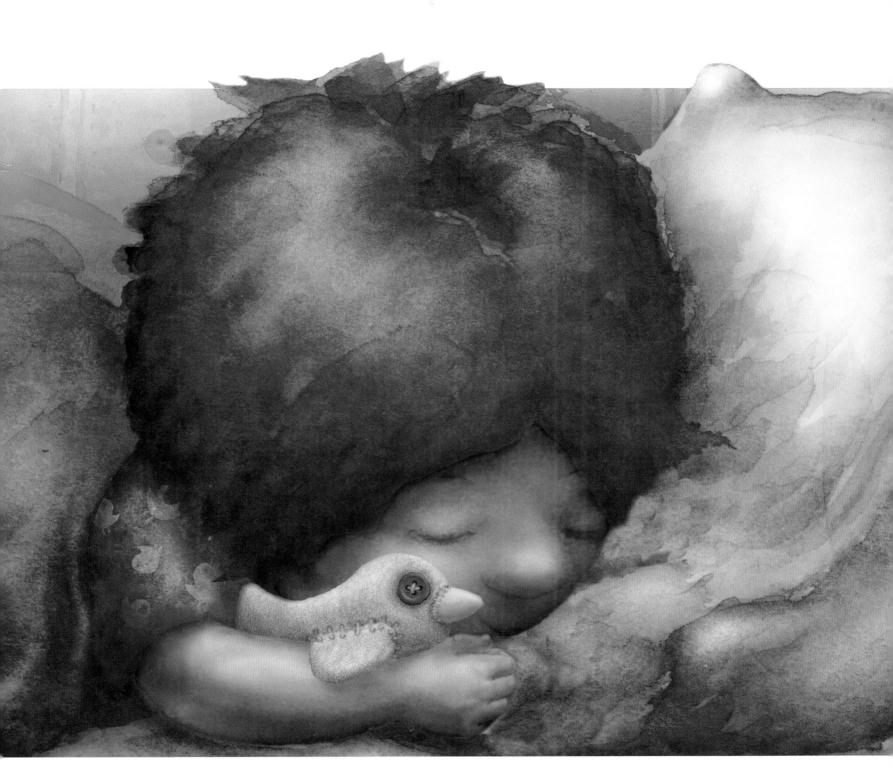

The End.